FAIRY TALE CLASSICS

Hansel and Gretel

tiger tales

For Charlie and Leo with lots of love ~ J.C.
To my parents ~ M.M.

tiger tales
5 River Road, Suite 128, Wilton, CT 06897
Published in the United States 2018
Originally published in Great Britain 2018 by Little Tiger Press
Text adapted by Josephine Collins
Text copyright © 2018 Josephine Collins
Illustrations copyright © 2018 Marisa Morea
ISBN-13: 978-1-68010-107-2
ISBN-10: 1-68010-107-2
Printed in China
LTP/1400/2178/0318

For more insight and activities, visit us at www.tigertalesbooks.com

FAIRY TALE CLASSICS

Hansel and Gretel

adapted by *Josephine Collins*
Illustrated by *Marisa Morea*

tiger tales

Hansel and Gretel lived in a teeny tiny house
at the edge of a great forest with their father
and stepmother. Their father was a woodcutter,
but he was so poor, he never had
enough money for food.

"How will we feed the children?" he moaned.
He was a good man, and he didn't know that
their stepmother had a plan. A terrible plan . . . .

"Husband, we must take the children into the forest and leave them there. Then we can be rid of them!" she said.

"We can't!" spluttered the woodcutter, horrified. But his wife was determined to have her way.

She's so mean!

Don't worry! I know what to do!

Late that night, as everyone slept, Hansel crept outside. He filled his pockets with pebbles that were sparkling like silver coins in the moonlight.

The next morning, the family set off. Clever Hansel
dropped the shiny pebbles along the path as they went.
When they reached the middle of the forest,
their stepmother announced: "Your father
and I are going to chop wood.
You stay here."

We'll be
back later.

But they didn't come back.

"I'm scared, Hansel!" cried Gretel.

But Hansel knew what to do.

Don't worry!
I have a plan!

When the moon came up, he took his little sister
by the hand, and they followed the glistening trail
of pebbles all the way home.

Their father was delighted to see them, but their stepmother said angrily: "You lazybones! Why did you sleep so long in the woods?"

That night, she nagged her husband. "We must take them even deeper into the forest!"

But this time, when Hansel got up to collect pebbles, his stepmother had shut and locked the door.

The following day, Hansel knew what to expect.
He made a trail of crumbs from the tiny piece
of bread he had been given for breakfast.

"Sit tight, you two!" ordered their stepmother once they
reached the deepest, darkest part of the forest. "We're
going to . . . er . . . chop . . . *more* wood! We'll be back later!"

But by nightfall, no one had come for them.

"Don't worry," said Hansel. "We'll follow the trail home!"

Oh, I forgot about the birds!

But—oh, no! The children could not find a single crumb!

They walked for a night and a day,
but the children were hopelessly lost!
"I can't go on! I'm so tired and
so hungry," sighed Gretel.

Just then, Hansel spotted
a little house ahead . . . .

It was made entirely from
gingerbread, candy, and cakes!
The children could not believe
their eyes! They ran to the house
and grabbed delicious, sweet
handfuls of treats.

As they munched happily, an old woman
poked her head around the door. "Come inside
and stay with me, my dears!" she smiled.

The children entered the house
and immediately realized that they
had been tricked!
The old woman was
really a witch!

She locked up Hansel and forced
Gretel to clean and cook.

"You must cook for your brother," she cackled.
"He looks so tasty—I think one day I will eat him!"
Gretel was terrified.

Every day, the witch checked to see if Hansel was ready to eat.

And every day, clever Hansel fooled the witch. He knew she couldn't see well, so he held out a bone instead of his finger.

The witch couldn't figure out why
Hansel was still so thin.
"I can't wait any longer!" she snapped.
"I'm eating him now! Gretel, light the oven!"

"It won't light," said Gretel.

"How can that be?" snarled the witch. And she stuck her head inside the oven to light the flame herself.

Gretel saw her chance. With all her strength, she pushed the witch into the oven!

The witch tumbled into the oven, and that was the end of her!

"You saved us!" cried Hansel as he hugged his sister.

Now that the children were
free to explore the witch's house,
they discovered hidden gold and
sparkling jewels!

Laughing happily, they filled up
their pockets and headed home.

When they arrived, their father hugged them tightly. He had never forgiven himself for leaving the children. Thankfully, their wicked stepmother had left long ago.

From that day on, the woodcutter and his beloved children were richer than they ever could have dreamed and never went hungry again.

Josephine Collins

Josephine is a writer of children's short stories,
novelty picture books, and gift books for adults. When she's
not writing, she works as a picture book editor, mentoring new writers
at The Golden Egg Academy in England. Josephine lives in London
with her husband and two young sons.

Marisa Morea

Marisa is an illustrator based in Madrid, Spain. She graduated
with an MA in Illustration from EINA in Barcelona in 2009.
After working as an art director for several advertising agencies,
she decided to become a full-time illustrator. She has worked with
many international clients in the United States, Europe, and Singapore.
In her spare time, she enjoys yoga and classic movies.
She also loves jazz music, vintage clothing, and lemon pies!